LE CORDON BLEU
HOME COLLECTION
·SUMMER·

MEREHURST

contents

4
Gazpacho

6
Malaysian-style salad

8
Crab fritters with lime and ginger chutney

10
Caesar salad

12
Prawn salad with lime mayonnaise

14
Beef carpaccio with rocket and Parmesan

16
Mediterranean salad/Watercress salad

18
Salade niçoise

20
Pan-fried duck breast with citrus salad

22
Dressed crab

24
Oriental grilled poussins

26
Asparagus, artichoke and lobster salad

28
Tiger prawns with sautéed capsicums

30
Cold ratatouille with chicken

32
Lamb cutlets with pea fritters and garlic cream sauce

34
Salmon with a shallot and coriander vinaigrette

36
Chicken satay

38
Seared tuna with chickpea salad

40
Grilled lobster with a buttery Pernod sauce

42
Roasted salmon with a basil and capsicum sauce

44
Teriyaki chicken

46
Fish kebabs with pumpkin and zucchini chutney

48
Lamb fillets with coriander gravy

50
Chilled melon soup with eau-de-Cologne mint sorbet

52
Strawberries Romanoff

54
Blueberry and buttermilk sorbet

56
Lemon sabayonette with fresh berries

58
Fraisier

60
Gratin of summer berries

62
Chef's techniques

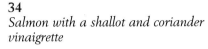

recipe ratings ❋ *easy* ❋❋ *a little more care needed* ❋❋❋ *more care needed*

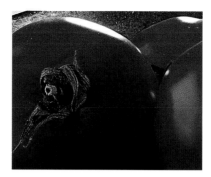

Gazpacho

Of Arabic origin, the name of this soup means 'soaked bread'. Gazpacho originates from Seville in the south of Spain, but many Spanish regions have their own versions of the soup.

Preparation time **35 minutes + 2 hours refrigeration**
Total cooking time **Nil**
Serves 6–8

GAZPACHO
75 g (2¹/₂ oz) fresh white bread, crusts removed
30 ml (1 fl oz) red wine vinegar
2 cloves garlic
³/₄ telegraph cucumber, unpeeled and roughly chopped
1 onion, chopped
¹/₂ green capsicum (pepper), roughly chopped
1.75 kg (3¹/₂ lb) ripe tomatoes, quartered and seeded
125 ml (4 fl oz) olive oil

TO GARNISH
¹/₄ telegraph cucumber, unpeeled
¹/₂ green capsicum (pepper)
4 slices of bread, crusts removed and toasted

1 In a food processor or blender, process the bread into fine breadcrumbs and add the vinegar, garlic, cucumber, onion, capsicum, tomato and a teaspoon of salt. Purée and then push through a sieve.

2 Return to the food processor or blender and pour in the olive oil in a thin steady stream. Alternatively, pour the mixture into a large bowl and briskly stir or whisk in the oil.

3 Check the flavouring, season with salt and freshly ground black pepper and add a little more vinegar if required for a refreshing tang. Check the consistency— the soup should be thinnish, so you may need to add a little more water to dilute it. Cover the bowl with two layers of plastic wrap and chill in the refrigerator for at least 2 hours.

4 To prepare the garnish, cut the remaining cucumber in half lengthways and use the point of a teaspoon to scoop out the seeds. Cut the cucumber, capsicum and bread into small cubes.

5 Pour the soup into well-chilled bowls and pass round the cucumber, capsicum and croutons in separate dishes for each person to sprinkle onto their own soup.

Chef's tips To serve, you could add two or three ice cubes to chill the soup, or for more colour, chop a red capsicum along with the green.

Make the soup a day in advance for a mature, well-rounded flavour, but cover it well, as the soup has a strong smell that can affect other foods in the refrigerator.

Malaysian-style salad

Tangy, sweet and crisp, this salad makes a delightful accompaniment to many Asian dishes. Experiment by using a variety of fruits and vegetables such as mangoes, grapefruit, starfruit or cucumber.

*Preparation time **40 minutes + 1 hour 10 minutes
  standing***
*Total cooking time **5 minutes***
Serves 6–8 people as a side dish

VINAIGRETTE
1–2 fresh red chillies
1 tablespoon soft brown sugar or honey
60 ml (2 fl oz) rice vinegar
3 teaspoons sesame oil
1 teaspoon light soy sauce (see Chef's tip)
1 teaspoon finely grated fresh ginger

1 medium ripe pineapple, peeled and trimmed
2 carrots
2 kiwi fruit
1 yellow capsicum (pepper)
1 red capsicum (pepper)
300 g (10 oz) snow peas (mangetout)
1 tablespoon shredded coconut

1 To make the vinaigrette, thinly slice or roughly chop the chillies. Place them in a non-metallic bowl or jar and add the sugar or honey, rice vinegar, sesame oil, soy sauce and ginger. Mix well and check the seasoning. Set aside at room temperature for at least 1 hour, or refrigerate overnight. Stir or shake occasionally.

2 Cut the pineapple into six to eight wedges. Remove and discard the core, then cut each wedge into 1 cm (1/2 inch) pieces. Slice the carrots at an angle to the same size as the pineapple. Peel the kiwi fruit, cut in half lengthways, then cut into 5 mm (1/4 inch) slices. Cut the capsicums into bite-size chunks.

3 Bring 2 litres water to the boil. Salt the water well, then blanch the snow peas for about 90 seconds. Rinse well with cold water and drain. Cut the snow peas in half at an angle, to the size of the other vegetables.

4 Reserve some shredded coconut for the garnish; mix the remainder into the vinaigrette and soak for 5–10 minutes. Toss the fruit and vegetables together in a large bowl with the vinaigrette. Sprinkle with the reserved coconut and serve immediately.

Chef's tip Light soy sauce is paler and milder than regular soy sauce, and is preferred in some recipes as it will not affect the colour and flavour of the dish. If it is hard to obtain, use 1/2 teaspoon salt instead.

Crab fritters with lime and ginger chutney

These warm crab and herb fritters are served with a tangy chutney which may be made well in advance. They could also be served with a dipping sauce made of mayonnaise, yoghurt and lime.

Preparation time **50 minutes + cooling**
Total cooking time **1 hour 10 minutes**
Makes about 12

LIME AND GINGER CHUTNEY
4 limes
juice of 1/2 lemon
juice of 1 orange
1 onion, sliced
1 clove garlic, crushed
3 teaspoons grated fresh ginger
pinch of saffron threads or powder
1 bay leaf
2–3 cloves
100 ml (31/4 fl oz) white wine vinegar
80 g (23/4 oz) soft brown sugar
50 g (13/4 oz) sultanas, soaked in 1 tablespoon brandy
1 teaspoon tomato paste

CRAB FRITTERS
150–200 g (5–61/2 oz) fresh breadcrumbs
250 g (8 oz) skinned white fish fillets, such as whiting, sole or haddock
1 egg white
100 ml (31/4 fl oz) thick (double) cream
250 g (8 oz) cooked white crab meat, shredded
30 g (1 oz) chopped mixed fresh herbs, such as dill, chives, parsley and tarragon
oil, for deep-frying

1   To make the lime and ginger chutney, peel the limes and remove the pith using a small sharp knife. Cut the limes into segments by making an incision on both sides of each segment towards the centre of the fruit, lifting out each lime segment as you work. Set aside. Squeeze the remaining juice from the empty membranes, add it to the lemon and orange juice and place in a pan with all the chutney ingredients except the lime segments. Simmer for 45–55 minutes, or until the mixture is almost dry, stirring frequently. Allow to cool slightly, then add the lime segments and leave the chutney to cool completely.

2   Sprinkle the breadcrumbs onto a sheet of greaseproof paper. To make the crab fritters, purée the fish in a food processor. Add the egg white, season with salt and pepper, and process again until well blended. Using the 'pulse' button or an on/off action, carefully add the cream—do not overwork or it will separate.

3   Transfer the mixture to a bowl, then set the bowl in a bowl of ice. Using a large metal spoon or plastic spatula, fold in the crab meat and mixed herbs. Using two tablespoons, shape the mixture into small ovals about 5 x 3 cm (2 x 11/4 inches) in size. Gently roll in the breadcrumbs to coat, using the paper to help toss the crumbs and to avoid handling the mixture.

4   Preheat a deep-fat fryer or deep pan, one-third full of oil, to 160°C (315°F). The oil is the right temperature when a cube of bread dropped into the oil browns in 30 seconds. Cook the fritters in batches for 4–6 minutes, or until golden brown all over, turning with a long-handled metal spoon. Drain on crumpled paper towels. Season with salt and serve warm with the chutney.

Chef's tips Once shaped and coated, the fritters can be refrigerated for up to 24 hours before deep-frying.

The chutney can be served as soon as it has cooled, or may be left to mature for up to 2 weeks in an airtight container in the refrigerator. You can also serve this chutney with cold meat, terrines or pâtés.

Caesar salad

This salad is often thought of as an American dish, but was actually created by Caesar Cardini in Tijuana, Mexico in the 1920s.

Preparation time **20 minutes**
Total cooking time **15 minutes**
Serves 4

DRESSING
2 egg yolks
I tablespoon lemon juice, or to taste
160 ml (5¼ fl oz) olive oil
4 anchovy fillets, finely chopped
2 cloves garlic, finely chopped

2 eggs
I head of cos lettuce
4 slices of white bread, crusts removed
80 ml (2¾ fl oz) olive oil
35 g (1¼ oz) Parmesan, freshly grated
2 tablespoons finely chopped fresh parsley

1 To make the dressing, beat the egg yolks and lemon juice using a whisk or blender. Add the oil in a thin steady stream and beat until thick and smooth. Stir through the anchovies and garlic and season to taste with salt, pepper and extra lemon juice. Set aside.
2 To hard-boil the eggs, place them in a small saucepan and cover with cold water. Bring to a gentle boil and cook for 10 minutes. Drain and cool in cold water, then peel and chop finely.
3 Tear the lettuce into bite-size pieces and set aside in the refrigerator. To make the croutons, cut the bread into even cubes. Heat the oil in a frying pan and brown the bread until nicely golden. Remove and drain on crumpled paper towels.
4 In a large serving bowl, toss the lettuce in the dressing. Sprinkle with the remaining ingredients to serve.

Chef's tip To make the salad a meal in itself, try adding smoked duck breast, chicken or salmon.

Prawn salad with lime mayonnaise

To make the most of the natural flavours of this chilled salad, season with a light hand. A touch of cumin and a refreshing lime mayonnaise transforms a simple lunch into a taste of summer.

Preparation time **15 minutes + 30 minutes standing**
Total cooking time **Nil**
Serves 6

1 green cucumber
2 tablespoons salt
25 g (3/4 oz) cumin seeds, lightly toasted (see Chef's tip)
500 g (1 lb) peeled cooked prawns, deveined, drained and dried
juice and finely grated rind of 1 lime
125 g (4 oz) plain yoghurt
125 g (4 oz) mayonnaise
sprigs of fresh chervil, to garnish

1 Peel the cucumber, cut it in half lengthways and use a teaspoon to scrape out the seeds. Cut the flesh into long, thin strips, about 10 cm x 2.5 mm (4 x 1/8 inch). Place on a large plate, sprinkle with the salt and stand for 30 minutes. (The salt will draw out the water and concentrate the flavour.) Drain off the liquid, pat dry with paper towels and sprinkle with the cumin seeds.

2 Place the prawns in a bowl, add 1 or 2 teaspoons of lime juice to taste and stir to combine. Season to taste with salt and freshly ground pepper. Firmly pack the prawns into six ramekins or timbale moulds of 100 ml (31/4 fl oz) capacity, then set aside in the refrigerator.

3 In a small bowl, mix together the grated lime rind, yoghurt, mayonnaise and remaining lime juice to taste. Stir together until well combined.

4 To serve, turn out the moulds onto six chilled plates. Arrange the cucumber strips around the prawns, and drizzle some lime and yoghurt mayonnaise around. Sprinkle a little salt over the prawns if desired. Garnish with a sprig of chervil and serve chilled.

Chef's tip To toast cumin seeds, place them in a dry frying pan. Fry over moderate heat for about 2 minutes, or until fragrant, taking care not to let the seeds burn or they will become bitter.

Beef carpaccio with rocket and Parmesan

*Beef carpaccio is a classic Italian first course consisting of very thin slices of raw beef
served with a vinaigrette and often topped with onions, or capers as in this recipe.*

Preparation time **15 minutes + 30 minutes freezing**
Total cooking time **Nil**
Serves 4

**350 g (11¼ oz) beef fillet, tenderloin or shell steak
(see Chef's tips)**
40 ml (1¼ fl oz) lemon juice
50 ml (1¾ fl oz) extra virgin olive oil
100 g (3¼ oz) piece of Parmesan, at room temperature
100 g (3¼ oz) rocket leaves
3 tablespoons drained capers

1 To prepare the carpaccio, trim the beef well of fat
and sinew. Wrap tightly in plastic wrap and freeze for at
least 30 minutes, or until very firm but not rock-solid.
Remove the plastic wrap and using a very sharp, thin
knife, slice the meat as thinly as possible. Place each slice
between two layers of plastic wrap and lightly pound
the slices to flatten them.

2 Divide the beef between four plates, arranging the
slices in a single layer, overlapping them slightly. Cover
with plastic wrap and refrigerate until ready to serve.

3 To make the dressing, whisk together the lemon juice
and olive oil. Season to taste with salt and freshly
ground pepper and set aside.

4 Using a vegetable peeler, shave cheese curls from the
piece of Parmesan, allowing six shavings per plate. Set
aside until ready to use.

5 Just before serving, toss the rocket leaves in half the
dressing and arrange on the plates with the carpaccio.
Sprinkle with the Parmesan and capers. Drizzle with
the remaining dressing and serve at once with freshly
ground black pepper.

Chef's tips When making your own carpaccio, it is very
important to use a good-quality cut of very fresh meat.
Alternatively, for the thinnest possible slices of beef,
your butcher may be able to prepare the carpaccio for
you. Order the meat several days in advance for the day
you plan to serve it, and specify how you would like it
prepared. Ask your butcher to lay out the slices on a
sheet of plastic wrap for easier handling.

This recipe can be adjusted to taste by adding freshly
chopped herbs such as basil, as well as olives, anchovies
or roasted capsicums (peppers).

Mediterranean salad

Balsamic vinegar is an Italian vinegar that adds an exquisite flavour to this salad.

*Preparation time **30 minutes***
*Total cooking time **Nil***
Serves 4

DRESSING
80 ml (2³/4 fl oz) balsamic vinegar
160 ml (5¹/4 fl oz) olive oil
4 cloves garlic, finely chopped
25 g (³/4 oz) fresh basil leaves, finely chopped

4 tomatoes
2 ripe avocados
125 g (4 oz) mozzarella cheese, thinly sliced
60 g (2 oz) prosciutto, cut into thin strips

1   To make the dressing, pour the balsamic vinegar into a bowl and slowly whisk in the olive oil. Once the oil has been incorporated, mix in the finely chopped garlic and basil leaves and season with salt and freshly ground black pepper.
2   Using a sharp knife, remove the stem ends from the tomatoes. Slice the tomatoes into wedges and place in a large salad bowl. Dice the avocado into large cubes and add to the tomatoes. Add the mozzarella cheese slices and sprinkle with the prosciutto strips.
3   Add the dressing and gently mix together. Season to taste with salt and freshly ground pepper and serve at once with crusty bread.

Watercress salad

This is a refreshing salad with a light dressing that is simple and quick to prepare.

*Preparation time **20 minutes + 1 hour refrigeration***
*Total cooking time **Nil***
Serves 4

250 g (8 oz) watercress, washed, stems removed
180 g (5³/4 oz) cherry tomatoes
200 g (6¹/2 oz) feta cheese, cut into cubes
I red onion, thinly sliced
45 g (1¹/2 oz) green olives, pitted
45 g (1¹/2 oz) black olives, pitted

DRESSING
2 cloves garlic, finely chopped
40 ml (1¹/4 fl oz) lemon juice
50 ml (1³/4 fl oz) olive oil

1   Place all the salad ingredients in a large serving bowl. Cover and refrigerate for 1 hour, or until well chilled.
2   To make the dressing, whisk together all the dressing ingredients. Add to the salad, toss well, and season to taste with salt and freshly ground pepper.

Chef's tips Be careful when adding salt to this salad as the olives and feta cheese already contain a lot of salt.

When using raw onions in a salad, remember they are milder in summer and stronger in winter. If an onion seems too strong to use raw, soak the slices in salted water for about 30 minutes, then rinse well before using.

Mediterranean salad (bottom) with Watercress salad

Salade niçoise

Salade niçoise is a typical southern dish from Nice, usually containing tomatoes, tuna and black olives. Originally this salad did not include cooked vegetables, but as it began to appear on menus around France, local chefs made their own adaptations, including the addition of potatoes.

*Preparation time **40 minutes + 20 minutes cooling***
*Total cooking time **1 hour 20 minutes***
Serves 4

200 ml (6¹/₂ fl oz) olive oil
1 bay leaf
4 sprigs of fresh thyme
1 piece of fresh tuna, about 400 g (12³/₄ oz), skin removed
300 g (10 oz) waxy or salad potatoes
240 g (7¹/₂ oz) green beans
50 ml (1³/₄ fl oz) white wine vinegar
1 green capsicum (pepper), cut into julienne strips (see Chef's tip)
1 red capsicum (pepper), cut into julienne strips
2 red onions, thinly sliced
1 bibb or butter lettuce
4 tomatoes, cut into quarters
4 hard-boiled eggs, shelled and quartered
50 g (1³/₄ oz) can anchovies, drained
30 black olives

1 Preheat the oven to slow 150°C (300°F/Gas 2). In a small pan, place the oil, bay leaf, thyme and tuna. Warm over low heat for 5 minutes, then place in the oven for 30 minutes, or until the tuna feels firm to the touch. Leave to cool for 20 minutes in the oil, remove the tuna and place on a rack to drain. Strain the oil and set aside.

2 Put the unpeeled potatoes in cold, salted water. Bring to the boil and cook for 30–35 minutes, or until the tip of a knife easily pierces them. Remove from the water and leave to cool. Peel, then slice into thick rounds.

3 Trim the beans and cook in boiling salted water for 8 minutes, or until tender. Refresh in cold water and drain.

4 To make the vinaigrette, whisk the vinegar and some salt together, then gradually whisk in the reserved oil.

5 Toss the potatoes, green beans, capsicums and onion with a little vinaigrette and season to taste with salt and black pepper. Break the tuna into bite-size pieces and mix with some of the vinaigrette. Arrange a few leaves of lettuce on each plate. In the centre, place a mound of the potatoes. Top with the green beans, capsicums and onion and finish with the tuna. Alternate the tomato and egg quarters around the edge and finish with the anchovies and olives. Serve the remaining vinaigrette on the side or drizzle over the salad just before serving.

Chef's tip Julienne strips are strips of vegetables, the size and shape of matchsticks.

Pan-fried duck breast with citrus salad

*The rich flavours of juicy duck are balanced perfectly in this dish by the refreshing bite
of citrus. Although simple to prepare, this wonderful meal is worthy of special occasions.*

*Preparation time **20 minutes***
*Total cooking time **35 minutes***
Serves 4

☙ ☙

2 oranges
2 grapefruit
125 g (4 oz) caster sugar
75 ml (2 1/2 fl oz) corn oil
3 tablespoons vegetable oil
4 duck breasts, about 180 g (5 3/4 oz) each
1 small head of radicchio lettuce
1/2 small curly endive
1/2 small oak leaf lettuce

1 Using a vegetable peeler, peel the rind from one orange and one grapefruit, avoiding the white pith. If there is any pith on the underside of the peel, remove it with a sharp knife to leave only the coloured rind. Cut the rind into very fine shreds and place in a pan with enough cold water to cover well. Bring to the boil, reduce the heat and simmer for 1 minute. Drain.

2 In a small pan, dissolve the sugar in 250 ml (8 fl oz) water over low heat. Bring to the boil, then reduce the heat, add the shredded rind and simmer for 8 minutes, or until candied—they will be soft and sweet. Lift out with a fork and spread over an upturned metal sieve to drain and cool. Finely grate the rind of the remaining orange and grapefruit and set aside in a small bowl.

3 Using a small sharp knife, cut away the white pith from the two oranges and grapefruit. Cut the fruit into segments by making an incision on both sides of each segment towards the centre of the fruit, lifting out each segment as you proceed. Set the segments aside. Squeeze 2–3 tablespoons of juice from the empty fruit membranes into the bowl with the grated rind. Slowly add the corn oil, whisking vigorously until the dressing has emulsified, then season to taste with salt and freshly ground pepper.

4 Heat the vegetable oil in a shallow pan. Trim the fat from the duck breasts and ensure all the feather stubs have been removed. Cook the duck, skin-side-up, for 6–8 minutes, or until golden brown. Turn and cook the skin side for 10–15 minutes, or until the flesh is just pink. Remove from the pan and rest in a warm place.

5 Drain the excess fat from the pan and allow the pan to cool slightly. Add the dressing to the pan, scraping well with a wooden spoon to mix in the pan juices.

6 Tear the salad leaves into bite-size pieces and toss them in some of the dressing, then pile them to the side of each serving plate. Slice the duck into diagonal slices about 5 mm (1/4 inch) thick, and arrange the slices in a semicircle around the other edge of the plate. Arrange the fruit segments on the plate, spoon any remaining dressing over the duck and sprinkle with a little of the candied peel.

Chef's tips When available, use a pink grapefruit instead of one of the yellow grapefruit in this recipe. Pink grapefruit has a lovely flavour and colour.

If you are buying pre-prepared mixed salad leaves, allow about 45 g (1 1/2 oz) per serving.

Dressed crab

In Britain, the most traditional way to enjoy fresh crab is to 'dress' it. This enduring favourite is well worth the effort and evokes the feeling of an old-fashioned, English seaside holiday.

Preparation time **40 minutes**
Total cooking time **10 minutes**
Serves 1–2

2 eggs, at room temperature
1 cooked crab, about 750 g–1 kg (1½–2 lb)
  (see Chef's tips)
1–2 tablespoons mayonnaise, to taste
60–100 g (2–3¼ oz) fresh breadcrumbs
Worcestershire or Tabasco sauce, to taste
3 tablespoons chopped fresh parsley
2–3 anchovy fillets, to garnish
2–3 teaspoons drained capers, to garnish
15 g (½ oz) stuffed green olives, sliced, to garnish
2–4 slices brown bread
20 g (¾ oz) unsalted butter, at room temperature
1 lime or lemon, cut into wedges

1 To hard-boil the eggs, place them in a small saucepan and cover with cold water. Bring to a gentle boil and cook for 10 minutes. Drain and cool in cold water. Peel the eggs and push the whites and the yolks separately through a fine sieve.

2 Prepare the crab, following the method in the Chef's techniques on page 63. Scrape all the creamy brown meat from the shell and sieve it into a bowl. Stir in the mayonnaise and breadcrumbs to bind, adding more of each if the flavour of the dark meat is too strong. Season with salt, freshly ground pepper and Worcestershire or Tabasco sauce.

3 Crack open the claws and remove all the white meat, checking that there are no shell splinters left (see Chef's tips). Season to taste.

4 Place the white meat from the claws and body of the crab towards the two outer sides of the cleaned and dried shell. Spoon the brown meat into the centre, then arrange the chopped parsley on the seams in between. Cover half of the white meat with the egg white; spoon the egg yolk on the dark meat. Garnish with anchovies, capers and sliced olives. Butter the bread thinly, and serve the dressed crab with the bread and lime or lemon wedges to the side.

Chef's tips When choosing a crab, select one that feels heavier than it looks. If possible, buy a fresh crab, as frozen crabs lose a lot of flavour and liquid as they defrost. Male crabs have larger claws than females.

The best way to check there are no shell splinters in the meat is to throw pinches of the meat onto a baking tray. Listen for the sound of shell pieces: if you do hear any, discard the meat.

Oriental grilled poussins

In this dish, an Asian-style marinade transforms delicately flavoured young chickens into something very special. Marinating them overnight will make them even more tender and succulent.

Preparation time **45 minutes + overnight marinating**
Total cooking time **40 minutes**
Serves 4

MARINADE
4 stalks lemon grass, white part only, halved
25 g (³/4 oz) fresh coriander leaves, stems and roots, chopped
4 French shallots, peeled and quartered
8 cloves garlic, peeled
100 g (3¹/4 oz) fresh ginger, peeled and chopped
60 g (2 oz) grated palm sugar or brown sugar
2 tablespoons curry powder
2 teaspoons ground black pepper
2 teaspoons salt
80 ml (2³/4 fl oz) fish sauce
500 ml (16 fl oz) can unsweetened coconut milk

2 poussins (baby chickens), each 600–750 g (1¹/4–1¹/2 lb)
2 tablespoons oil

1 To make the marinade, very finely chop the lemon grass, coriander, shallots, garlic and ginger in a blender or small food processor. Add the sugar, curry powder, pepper, salt and fish sauce and process for 30 seconds. With the machine still running, add 125 ml (4 fl oz) of the coconut milk. Process until smooth, then transfer to a shallow, non-metallic bowl.

2 Cut the baby chickens in half and toss them in the marinade to coat well all over. Cover and refrigerate overnight, turning once or twice.

3 Preheat the oven to very hot 230°C (450°F/Gas 8). Coat the base of a baking dish with the oil. Reserving the marinade, place the chickens in the dish and bake for 25–30 minutes, turning three or four times.

4 Transfer the reserved marinade to a saucepan and mix in the remaining coconut milk. Place over medium heat and bring to a gentle boil. Simmer for 5 minutes, then strain. Season to taste and keep warm. Serve the marinade over the chicken or on the side.

Chef's tip Coriander stems have a more intense flavour than the leaves, and are often used for marinades.

Asparagus, artichoke and lobster salad

This is an elegant salad for a special occasion. The walnut oil adds a delicious nutty flavour to the dressing, but don't be tempted to increase the quantity as it has a strong flavour.

*Preparation time **1 hour + chilling***
*Total cooking time **35 minutes***
Serves 4

COURT BOUILLON
1 large carrot, finely sliced
2 onions, finely sliced
2 celery sticks, finely sliced
1 leek, white part only, finely sliced
3 sprigs of fresh thyme
1 bay leaf
10 black peppercorns
500 ml (16 fl oz) white wine
3 tablespoons salt

3 uncooked lobster tails
24 stalks asparagus
4 tablespoons salt, extra

DRESSING
60 ml (2 fl oz) sherry vinegar
1 French shallot, finely chopped
60 ml (2 fl oz) walnut oil
120 ml (4 fl oz) vegetable oil
1 tablespoon chopped fresh chervil or chives

4 large artichoke hearts, from a jar or can
20 whole fresh chervil leaves, to garnish

1 To make the court bouillon, place all the vegetables with the thyme sprigs, bay leaf, peppercorns and wine in a large pot and bring to the boil. Cook for 5 minutes over high heat. Add the salt and 4 litres water and return to the boil. Add the lobster tails, bring to the boil and cook for 12 minutes. Remove the pot from the heat and allow the lobster to cool slightly.

2 When the lobster is cool enough to handle, remove it from the bouillon. Discard the bouillon. Remove the tail in a single piece, following the method in the Chef's techniques on page 63, then slice into medallions. Cover and refrigerate.

3 Wash the asparagus under cold, running water. Using a small knife, remove the spurs from the asparagus stems, starting from the top and working down, then remove the outer layer from the lower two thirds of the stem using a vegetable peeler. Lining up the tips, tie the stalks in bundles of six to eight, following the method in the Chef's techniques on page 63.

4 Bring 4 litres water to the boil. Add the extra salt and then the asparagus bundles. Reduce the heat to a gentle simmer and cook for 5–8 minutes, or until the tips are tender. Remove the bundles and plunge into iced water, then drain on paper towels. Remove the strings, place in a bowl, cover and refrigerate.

5 To make the dressing, whisk together the vinegar and shallot. Gradually whisk in the oils, then the chervil or chives. Season and set aside. Rinse the artichokes well, pat dry, toss them in a little dressing and season to taste. Repeat with the asparagus, being careful not to break the tips. Refrigerate the vegetables until ready to use. To serve, arrange the artichokes, asparagus and lobster medallions on serving plates. Drizzle the remaining dressing around the artichoke, then garnish with chervil.

Chef's tip The cooked lobster tail shells can be frozen and used another time when preparing a seafood bisque or broth.

Tiger prawns with sautéed capsicums

This colourful dish is perfect as a starter or a light main course. It derives its superb flavour from the sweetness of the capsicums, spiked with lemon oil and fresh ginger.

Preparation time **30 minutes + 1 hour infusion**
Total cooking time **5 minutes**
Serves 4

LEMON OIL
60 ml (2 fl oz) oil
finely grated rind of 1/4 lemon

1.25 kg (2 lb 8 oz) raw large tiger or king prawns
1 red capsicum (pepper)
1 yellow capsicum (pepper)
1 tablespoon grated fresh ginger
1 tablespoon crushed garlic
60 ml (2 fl oz) dry sherry
2 tablespoons lemon juice
2 teaspoons light soy sauce

1 To make the lemon oil, gently warm the oil until lukewarm. Add the lemon rind, then leave the oil to cool and infuse for 1 hour. Strain before using.

2 Leaving the heads attached, remove the shells and tails from the prawns. Remove the eyes. With a small knife, make a shallow cut along the back of each prawn and carefully remove the dark vein. Pat the prawns dry on paper towels.

3 Cut the capsicums in half and remove the stems and seeds. Dice into 5 mm (1/4 inch) cubes and set aside.

4 Heat the lemon oil in a wok over high heat until it begins to smoke. Add the ginger, garlic and capsicum and stir-fry for 1 minute, then add the prawns and stir-fry for 1 minute more. Stir in the sherry, lemon juice and soy sauce and stir-fry for about 3 minutes, or until the prawns are just tender. Serve the prawns hot, with fresh crusty bread and a crisp green salad.

Cold ratatouille with chicken

Ratatouille is a French Provençal vegetable stew, originally from Nice. In this recipe it is served cold and is therefore best prepared the day before serving.

*Preparation time **45 minutes + overnight refrigeration***
*Total cooking time **1 hour 20 minutes***
Serves 4

RATATOUILLE
olive oil, for cooking
1 red capsicum (pepper), cut into short strips
250 g (8 oz) zucchini (courgette), cut into short strips
250 g (8 oz) eggplant (aubergine), cut into short strips
1 onion, chopped
400 g (12³/4 oz) tomatoes, peeled, seeded and chopped
2 cloves garlic, chopped
bouquet garni (see page 63)
15 g (¹/2 oz) bunch fresh basil, leaves trimmed and chopped

extra olive oil, for cooking
4 skinless chicken breast fillets
2 tablespoons lemon juice
1 sprig of fresh thyme

1 Preheat the oven to slow 150°C (300°F/Gas 2). To make the ratatouille, heat 1–2 tablespoons of oil in a deep, ovenproof frying pan. Sauté the capsicum strips for 2–3 minutes over medium-high heat. Remove and drain on paper towels.

2 Add some more oil to the pan and sauté the zucchini and eggplant separately, adding oil as needed and removing the vegetables to drain on paper towels. Add the onion and cook without colouring over medium-low heat for 3–5 minutes, or until soft. Add the tomatoes and garlic and cook over low heat, stirring occasionally, for 3 minutes, or until the moisture evaporates.

3 Add the drained vegetables and bouquet garni, then cover and bake for 30 minutes. Remove the bouquet garni, stir in the chopped basil and season to taste with salt and freshly ground black pepper. Allow to cool completely, then refrigerate overnight.

4 Heat 2 tablespoons of oil over medium-low heat in a frying pan. Season the chicken breasts with salt and freshly ground pepper, then cook them in a single layer for about 5 minutes on each side, or until browned and just cooked through. Transfer to a wire rack to cool.

5 Drain the pan of excess oil and add the lemon juice with 125 ml (4 fl oz) water. Return to the heat and add the thyme. Stir well, scraping the base of the pan to dissolve the cooking juices. Transfer the sauce to a small saucepan and gently simmer for 10 minutes. Season to taste. Strain and set aside to cool.

6 To serve, divide the cold ratatouille between four plates, slice the chicken breasts and arrange around the ratatouille. Drizzle the cooled sauce over the top.

Chef's tip If you are planning to serve a dish cold, season it well during cooking, as chilling can dull the flavours.

Lamb cutlets with pea fritters and garlic cream sauce

Lean pink lamb cutlets served with bright green pea fritters and a creamy garlic sauce make an unusual, appetizing and colourful summer's meal.

*Preparation time **35 minutes + 40 minutes refrigeration***
*Total cooking time **1 hour***
Serves 4

I teaspoon salt
800 g (I lb 10 oz) peas, fresh or frozen
10 g (1/4 oz) unsalted butter
I egg yolk
2 teaspoons finely chopped fresh mint leaves
seasoned flour, for coating
2 eggs
60 g (2 oz) blanched almonds, finely chopped
60 g (2 oz) dried breadcrumbs
oil, for deep-frying
12 lamb cutlets, trimmed of excess fat
30 g (I oz) unsalted butter, melted

GARLIC CREAM SAUCE
10 cloves garlic, halved
100 ml (3 1/4 fl oz) white wine (not too dry)
300 ml (10 fl oz) thick (double) cream

1 Half-fill a medium pan with water and bring to the boil. Add the salt and peas, return to the boil, then reduce the heat and simmer for 3 minutes, or until the peas are tender. Drain well, then purée the peas in a food processor. Push the purée through a fine sieve to remove the skins.

2 Melt the butter in a small pan, add the pea purée and cook over low heat for about 7 minutes, or until the mixture is dry. Remove from the heat, stir in the egg yolk and chopped mint, and season with salt and freshly ground pepper. Leave to cool, then refrigerate for about 20 minutes, or until firm.

3 Place the seasoned flour on a sheet of greaseproof paper. Beat the eggs in a shallow bowl. Mix together the almonds and breadcrumbs and place them on another sheet of greaseproof paper. Divide the pea mixture into 12 portions and roll each portion between your palms into a ball, or shape them into patties. Coat the fritters with the flour, dip them in the beaten egg and then roll them in the almond mixture. Refrigerate for 20 minutes.

4 To make the garlic cream sauce, place the garlic in a small pan, cover with cold water and bring to the boil. Reduce the heat and simmer for 3 minutes, then drain. Return the garlic to the pan, add the white wine and cream, then cover and simmer gently for about 25 minutes, or until the garlic is soft. Pour the garlic mixture into a food processor or blender and process until smooth. Transfer to a clean pan to keep warm and season to taste. Preheat the grill to high, and set the oven to its lowest setting.

5 Preheat a deep-fat fryer or deep pan, one-third full of oil, to 180°C (350°F). Deep-fry the fritters in small batches, stirring gently to ensure even browning. When they are nicely golden, remove the fritters and drain on crumpled paper towels. Place on a wire rack and keep warm in the oven.

6 Brush the lamb cutlets with the melted butter and season with salt and freshly ground pepper. Grill for 3 minutes on each side for pink, or longer if preferred.

7 Divide the cutlets and fritters between warm serving plates and serve with a little garlic cream sauce.

Salmon with a shallot and coriander vinaigrette

Here, a fresh salmon fillet is drizzled with a deliciously sharp vinaigrette, and for a light summery meal requires little more than a serving of new potatoes, or a crisp green salad.

Preparation time 15 minutes
Total cooking time 20 minutes
Serves 4

SHALLOT AND CORIANDER VINAIGRETTE
50 ml (1³/4 fl oz) white wine vinegar
2 French shallots, finely chopped
1 teaspoon coriander seeds, crushed
100 ml (3¹/4 fl oz) white wine
1 tablespoon Noilly Prat or dry vermouth
75 ml (2¹/2 fl oz) fish stock
75 ml (2¹/2 fl oz) olive oil
3 tomatoes, peeled, seeded and diced into
* 5 mm (¹/4 inch) cubes*
30 g (1 oz) chopped fresh coriander leaves
1 teaspoon lemon juice, or to taste

4 salmon fillets, about 200 g (6¹/2 oz) each
30 g (1 oz) unsalted butter

1 To make the shallot and coriander vinaigrette, place the white wine vinegar, shallots and coriander seeds in a medium saucepan. Bring to the boil, then reduce the heat and simmer for 1 minute, or until reduced to a syrup. Add the wine and simmer for 3 minutes, or until reduced by two thirds. Stir in the alcohol and fish stock and simmer for 3 minutes, or until reduced by half. Season to taste, then remove from the heat and add the oil in a thin steady stream, whisking constantly until the sauce thickens and emulsifies. Strain and keep warm until ready to serve.

2 Season the salmon fillets on both sides with a little salt and freshly ground pepper. Melt the butter in a frying pan over medium heat, then cook the salmon for 4–5 minutes on each side, or until cooked through.

3 To serve, add the chopped tomatoes, coriander leaves and lemon juice to the warm vinaigrette. Place each salmon fillet onto a hot serving plate and drizzle with some warm vinaigrette. If you like, sprinkle the salmon with a little chopped fresh dill or coriander.

Chicken satay

Satay, an Indonesian dish, consists of skewered strips of marinated and grilled meat served with a smooth peanut sauce. Satays are a superb party snack, but make plenty as they disappear quickly!

*Preparation time **35 minutes + 30 minutes soaking + 2 hours marinating***
*Total cooking time **5–6 minutes per batch***
Serves 6

MARINADE
1/2 teaspoon ground anise seed (see Chef's tips)
1/2 teaspoon ground cumin
1 1/2 teaspoons ground turmeric
1 1/2 teaspoons ground coriander
2 French shallots, chopped
1 clove garlic, finely chopped
2.5 cm (1 inch) piece fresh ginger, finely chopped
2 stalks lemon grass, white part only, finely chopped
40 g (1 1/4 oz) soft brown sugar
70 ml (2 1/4 fl oz) peanut oil
2 teaspoons soy sauce

6 skinless chicken breast fillets

SATAY SAUCE
1 clove garlic
80 g (2 3/4 oz) smooth peanut butter
2 tablespoons coconut milk
a few drops of Tabasco, or to taste
2 tablespoons honey
2 tablespoons lemon juice
2 tablespoons soy sauce

1 Soak 25 wooden skewers in water for 30 minutes. Combine all the marinade ingredients, mix thoroughly and set aside.

2 Cut the chicken into 5 mm (1/4 inch) strips and thread them onto the soaked skewers. Place in a shallow dish and thoroughly coat with the marinade. Cover and refrigerate for 2 hours.

3 To make the satay sauce, place the garlic in a small pan. Cover with water, bring to the boil, then reduce the heat and simmer for about 3 minutes. Refresh the garlic under cold water, drain well, then crush. Return the garlic to the pan with the peanut butter, coconut milk and 60 ml (2 fl oz) water, then stir over medium heat for 1–2 minutes, or until smooth and thick. Add all the remaining sauce ingredients and stir well until warmed through. If the sauce starts to separate, stir in a little water.

4 Preheat the grill to high. When the grill is hot, grill the chicken in batches for 5–6 minutes, turning three or four times. Remove and cover with foil while cooking the remaining chicken, then transfer to a serving tray. Serve the sauce separately.

Chef's tips Anise seed is also known as sweet cumin.

Pre-packed ground spices tend to lose flavour during storage, so for special occasions you may like to grind your own. Simply fry the whole spices separately in a dry frying pan, then process them in a food processor, or pound them into a powder using a mortar and pestle.

Seared tuna with chickpea salad

These tuna steaks are infused with Oriental flavours and are seared quickly to great effect.
The chickpea salad is very versatile, and is also lovely with grilled vegetables or chicken.

*Preparation time **10 minutes + overnight soaking +***
*   **+ 3–4 hours marinating***
*Total cooking time **1 hour 5 minutes***
Serves 4

125 g (4 oz) dried chickpeas (see Chef's tip)
4 tuna steaks
1 bay leaf
1 French shallot, chopped
1 small clove garlic, crushed
1 red chilli, seeded and chopped
1 red capsicum (pepper), chopped
1 avocado
2 tablespoons chopped fresh coriander leaves
4 lime wedges, to serve

MARINADE
100 ml (3¼ fl oz) olive oil
finely grated rind and juice of 1½ limes
6 stalks of fresh coriander, roughly chopped or
**   slightly bruised**

1 Soak the chickpeas overnight in plenty of cold water.
2 Combine the marinade ingredients and mix well. Place the tuna steaks in a shallow glass or ceramic dish and pour on a third of the marinade, turning to coat both sides. Cover with plastic wrap and refrigerate for 3–4 hours, turning the tuna occasionally.
3 Drain the chickpeas and place in a large pan with enough water to cover. Add the bay leaf, bring to the boil, then reduce the heat and simmer for 1 hour, or until tender. Drain and set aside.
4 To make the chickpea salad, place the chickpeas, shallot, garlic, chilli and capsicum in a bowl and toss well. Peel and dice the avocado and fold into the salad with the coriander. Strain the remaining marinade into the salad and season to taste.
5 Preheat the grill to high. When the grill is hot, cook the tuna for about 2 minutes on each side, or chargrill for 1 minute on each side. Serve on warmed plates with a wedge of lime, and the chickpea salad on the side.

Chef's tip To save time, you can use 250 g (8 oz) canned chickpeas. Drain well and add to the salad in step 4.

Grilled lobster with a buttery Pernod sauce

Seafood gains a wonderful new dimension when served with a buttery sauce brightened with a dash of Pernod. The aniseed flavour of the sauce is enhanced with the infusion of star anise.

Preparation time **15 minutes**
Total cooking time **30 minutes**
Serves 4

PERNOD SAUCE
1 star anise
2 tablespoons Pernod
200 g (6¹/2 oz) unsalted butter, cubed

4 raw lobster tails
40 g (1¹/4 oz) unsalted butter, melted

1 To make the Pernod sauce, place 125 ml (4 fl oz) water in a small pan with the star anise and bring to the boil. Reduce the heat to low and simmer for 10 minutes, or until reduced to about 2 tablespoons. Stir in half the Pernod. Whisking constantly, gradually add the butter, a few pieces at a time. Season with salt and ground white pepper, then place the pan in a bowl or pan of hot water to keep warm. (The sauce will separate if placed back over direct heat.)

2 Add the lobster tails to a large pot of boiling water and cook for 2 minutes, or until the shells turn bright orange. Drain and refresh in cold water.

3 Place the lobster tails on a cutting board with the soft undershells facing down. Using a large knife, but without cutting all the way through, split the tails in half lengthways down the back, then open them up.

4 Preheat the grill to high. Brush the lobster flesh with the melted butter, season lightly, then grill, cut-side-down, for 5 minutes. Turn and grill the other side for 5–10 minutes, or until the flesh is firm. Transfer to serving plates. Stir the remaining Pernod into the sauce, then spoon a little sauce over the tail and serve the remainder on the side.

Chef's tip You could also use cooked whole lobsters in this recipe. First remove the claws by twisting where they meet the body, then crack them using a nutcracker or meat mallet and set aside to serve later with the grilled lobsters.

   Place the lobsters face-down on a cutting board. Using a large knife, but without cutting all the way through, split the lobsters in half lengthways down the back, then open them up. Remove the vein along the tail, the small sac just behind the mouth, and any coral or grey-green liver (tomalley). Brush the flesh with melted butter, season lightly and grill under a hot grill until heated through, turning during cooking.

Roasted salmon with a basil and capsicum sauce

The smoky sweetness of roasted capsicum marries with peppery basil in this inspirational sauce which makes salmon fillets, simply cooked, so sumptuous. Enjoy in the garden with a glass of chilled wine.

Preparation time **15 minutes**
Total cooking time **8–12 minutes**
Serves **4**

2 red capsicums (peppers)
100 ml (3¹/4 fl oz) olive oil
4 salmon fillets, scaled but not skinned
30 ml (1 fl oz) vegetable oil
30 g (1 oz) unsalted butter
2 tablespoons fresh basil leaves, shredded

1 Preheat the oven to hot 220°C (425°F/Gas 7). Lightly brush the whole capsicums with some olive oil, then place them on a baking tray and roast for 15–20 minutes, or until the skin is blackened and blistered and the capsicums are soft. Cover them with plastic wrap, or place in a plastic bag. (The capsicums will sweat, making the skins peel off more easily.) Allow to cool. Peel away the skin, then halve and seed the capsicums.

2 To make the sauce, place the capsicum in a blender or food processor, add the remaining olive oil and work to a smooth purée. Season to taste with salt and freshly ground black pepper, and transfer to a small pan.

3 Season the salmon fillets with salt and freshly ground pepper. Heat the vegetable oil and butter in a flameproof dish over high heat. Place the salmon in the dish, skin-side-up, then transfer to the oven and bake for 2 minutes. Turn and bake for 6 minutes, or until the salmon is cooked through and the skin is lightly coloured.

4 Gently heat the sauce, then add the basil. Transfer the salmon to warm plates and pour the sauce around. Serve at once with a mixed green salad.

Teriyaki chicken

The name of this celebrated Japanese dish derives from the words 'teri' meaning to shine, and 'yaki' to grill. The chicken receives its appetizing glaze from the small quantity of sugar in the sauce.

Preparation time **40 minutes**
Total cooking time **35 minutes**
Serves 4

4 chicken Marylands (leg-quarters), boned (see page 62)
1 tablespoon oil
1 tablespoon chopped fresh coriander

TERIYAKI SAUCE
100 ml (3 1/4 fl oz) sake (see Chef's tips)
100 ml (3 1/4 fl oz) mirin (see Chef's tips)
100 ml (3 1/4 fl oz) dark soy sauce
1 tablespoon caster sugar
2 teaspoons finely chopped fresh ginger
1 tablespoon finely chopped garlic

1 Using a fork, pierce the chicken through the skin several times to allow the sauce to penetrate, and to prevent shrinkage during cooking. In a large, deep frying pan, heat a tablespoon of oil over medium-high heat. Brown the chicken, skin-side-down, for 3–5 minutes.

Reduce the heat to low, turn the chicken over, then cover and cook for 10 minutes. Transfer the chicken to a plate.

2 To make the teriyaki sauce, whisk together all the sauce ingredients until the sugar has dissolved. Pour into the pan and bring to the boil. Whisking constantly, boil for 2–3 minutes, or until thickened slightly. Return the chicken to the pan and cook for about 15 minutes, or until the sauce has reduced to a glossy syrup. You will need to turn the chicken several times to completely coat it with the sauce.

3 To serve, slice the chicken and drizzle with any remaining sauce. Sprinkle the coriander over the top.

Chef's tips Sake is a dry Japanese rice wine. Dry sherry can be used instead. Mirin is a mild Japanese rice wine. If it is not available, you could use cider vinegar instead and increase the sugar by 1 tablespoon.

The chicken can be grilled or barbecued, if you prefer. Marinate the chicken in the teriyaki sauce for at least 2 hours, then remove the chicken and boil the sauce for 2–3 minutes, or until thickened. Grill or barbecue the chicken, brushing it with the sauce.

Fish kebabs with
pumpkin and zucchini chutney

*These tangy, grilled mixed-fish kebabs are nicely complemented by a fresh-flavoured chutney,
which is best made a day ahead to allow the flavours to mature. If there is a little chutney
to spare, try serving it with cheese or cold meats.*

*Preparation time **20 minutes + overnight refrigeration
+ 30 minutes soaking + 30 minutes marinating***
*Total cooking time **1 hour 20 minutes***
*Serves **4–6***

PUMPKIN AND ZUCCHINI CHUTNEY
250 g (8 oz) firm-fleshed pumpkin, finely chopped
**250 g (8 oz) zucchini (courgette), diced into 1 cm
 (1/2 inch) cubes**
1 large onion, chopped
200 g (61/2 oz) soft brown sugar
100 ml (31/4 fl oz) white wine vinegar
1 tablespoon tomato paste

juice of 1/2 lemon
500 g (16 oz) salmon fillets, skinned
500 g (16 oz) swordfish or monkfish, skinned
juice of 1/2 lime
2 tablespoons chilli oil (see Chef's tip)

1 To make the pumpkin and zucchini chutney, place
the pumpkin in a pan with the zucchini, onion, sugar,
vinegar, tomato paste and 100 ml (31/4 fl oz) water.
Bring to the boil, stirring to dissolve the sugar. Reduce
the heat to low and simmer gently for 1 hour, or until
soft and pulpy—the liquid should evaporate, leaving
enough syrup to keep the mixture moist. Pour into a
bowl to cool, then cover and refrigerate overnight.

2 Place 12 wooden skewers in a shallow dish. Pour the
lemon juice over, adding a little cold water to just cover.
Leave for 30 minutes and drain well.

3 Cut the fish into 2 cm (3/4 inch) cubes, then thread
alternately onto the skewers and place in a shallow glass
or ceramic dish. Combine the lime juice and chilli oil
and pour over the kebabs, turning well to coat all sides.
Cover and refrigerate for 30 minutes.

4 Preheat the grill to high. When hot, grill the kebabs
for 5–8 minutes on each side, or until lightly golden and
cooked through. Serve hot with the chutney.

Chef's tip To make chilli oil, warm 500 ml (16 fl oz)
vegetable oil. Add 10 g (1/4 oz) of dried chillies. Remove
from the heat and infuse for 24 hours, then strain into a
sterilised bottle and store for up to 2 months in a cool,
dark place. Refrigerate in warmer climates.

Lamb fillets with coriander gravy

*Roasted pine nuts add a wonderful texture to these medallions of pink lamb, presented on
a bed of English spinach, with a syrupy sauce of shallots and herbs.*

*Preparation time **30 minutes***
*Total cooking time **30 minutes***
Serves 4

2 x 6-chop racks of lamb (best end of neck)
1 tablespoon oil or clarified butter
2 large French shallots, chopped
**500 ml (16 fl oz) lamb stock (see page 62) or light
beef stock**
25 g (3/4 oz) fresh coriander leaves, chopped
1 tablespoon fresh mint leaves, chopped
1 tablespoon hazelnut oil
**1.5 kg (3 lb) English spinach leaves, picked over
and washed**
**2 large tomatoes, peeled, seeded and diced into
5 mm (1/4 inch) cubes**
100 g (31/4 oz) pine nuts, toasted

1 Remove the 'eye' or long round fillet of meat at the
thick end of each rack by running a small, sharp knife
along the bone.

2 Heat the oil or clarified butter in a shallow pan.
Season the fillets with salt, then fry over gentle heat,

turning now and then, for 10–12 minutes, or until still
just pink inside, yet browned outside. Remove the fillets
from the pan; keep warm and leave to rest.

3 Drain the pan of any excess fat, then add the shallots
and cook for about 2 minutes, or until lightly coloured.
Add the stock, bring to the boil, then reduce the heat
and simmer rapidly for about 10 minutes, or until the
mixture is syrupy. Remove from the heat, adjust the
seasoning, then stir in the coriander and mint. Cover
and keep warm.

4 In another frying pan, heat the hazelnut oil and
quickly cook the whole spinach leaves over high heat
until just wilted. Drain and season to taste. Pack the
spinach into four flat 250 ml (4 fl oz) capacity moulds
or ramekins, then turn each mould out onto the centre
of a warm plate.

5 Carve the lamb fillets into medallions about 5 mm
(1/4 inch) thick. Arrange the medallions on the spinach
beds and swirl the sauce around; sprinkle the chopped
tomatoes and pine nuts over the sauce. Roast potatoes
are a wonderful accompaniment.

Chef's tip Ask your butcher to remove the fillets from
the racks of lamb for you.

Chilled melon soup
with eau-de-Cologne mint sorbet

While working at a hotel in the Channel Islands, a chef encountered an eau-de-Cologne mint growing in a walled garden. He was inspired to try the mint in a sorbet, and his wonderful creation became popularly known at the hotel as 'Sorbet 4711'.

Preparation time **15 minutes + 2 hours refrigeration**
   + churning
Total cooking time **5 minutes**
Serves 4

I Galia melon (see Chef's tips)
I kg (2 lb) watermelon, peeled and chopped
140 g (4¹/2 oz) caster sugar
40 g (1¹/4 oz) eau-de-Cologne mint, finely chopped
   (See Chef's tips)
juice of I lemon, or to taste

1 To make the melon soup, halve the Galia melon and remove the seeds. Scoop the flesh into a blender or food processor with the flesh from the watermelon (you don't need to remove the seeds). Process to a purée, then rub through a sieve into a bowl to remove the watermelon seeds. If the melons are slightly under-ripe you may need to add sugar or lemon juice to develop the flavour. Cover and refrigerate for 2 hours.
2 To make the mint sorbet, gently heat the sugar and 500 ml (16 fl oz) water in a small pan and stir to dissolve the sugar. Bring to the boil, then remove from the heat and leave to cool. Add the mint, and lemon juice to taste.
3 Pour the syrup into an ice-cream machine and churn until firm. (The churning time will vary depending on your machine.)
4 Ladle the soup into chilled bowls and spoon the sorbet into the centre. Serve immediately.

Chef's tips Rockmelon, Charentais melon or a ripe honeydew may be used instead of the Galia melon.

Eau-de-Cologne mint is also known as orange mint, although regular mint may also be used.

If you do not have an ice-cream machine, pour the mixture into a shallow metal container, freeze until crystals form, then whisk or stir with a fork and return to the freezer. Repeat until frozen evenly and firm.

As it is difficult to make a small quantity of sorbet, you will have some left over. Serve it between courses to cleanse the palate, or to accompany fruit, sweet courses or chocolate. The sorbet may be frozen in an airtight container for up to 1 week, but is best served freshly made.

Strawberries Romanoff

*Deceptively easy to prepare, this memorable dessert will leave a lasting impression
on your guests. Orange juice may be used in place of the liqueur.*

Preparation time **15 minutes + overnight refrigeration
+ 30 minutes chilling**
Total cooking time **10 minutes**
Serves 6

350 g (11¼ oz) fresh strawberries
60 g (2 oz) caster sugar
50 ml (1¾ fl oz) Kirsch or Grand Marnier
425 ml (13½ fl oz) thick (double) cream
a few drops of vanilla extract or essence
2 tablespoons apricot jam
100 g (3¼ oz) good-quality dark chocolate, chopped
rose leaves, washed and dried (optional)

1 Wash and thoroughly dry the strawberries and set
three aside for decoration. Remove the stalks from the
remaining strawberries. Roughly chop the fruit, place in
a bowl and add the caster sugar and liqueur. Toss well,
cover with plastic wrap and refrigerate overnight.
2 Mix the cream and vanilla and whisk lightly using
a hand whisk until the whisk just leaves a trail, yet
the cream still runs if the bowl is tipped. Add half the
strawberries and whisk to a firm peak. Spoon the
mixture into a piping bag without a nozzle.

3 Place the remaining strawberries into six 175 ml
(5¾ fl oz) capacity serving glasses. Pipe the cream
mixture onto the strawberries, to reach just below the
rim of the glass. Transfer to the refrigerator and chill for
30 minutes.
4 Bring the jam and 2 teaspoons water to the boil in
a small pan. Slice the reserved strawberries in half,
through the stalk. Brush the cut-side of each strawberry
with the melted glaze and set aside to cool. Decorate
each glass with a strawberry half.
5 Bring a small pan half-full of water to the boil, then
remove from the heat. Place the chocolate in a bowl
over the hot water, stirring gently until the chocolate has
melted. Brush a thick layer of chocolate onto the shiny
side of each rose leaf, then gently place on a tray lined
with baking paper and refrigerate for 5 minutes to set
the chocolate.
6 To serve, carefully peel the leaves from the paper and
place a chocolate leaf on each chilled dessert.

Chef's tips Any fresh berries may be used in this recipe.
For a family dinner, make the dessert in a large glass
serving bowl. For a very elegant dinner-party finish, you
could serve the Romanoff in store-bought chocolate
cups or brandy-snap baskets.

Blueberry and buttermilk sorbet

This refreshing sorbet is a perfect palate cleanser after a heavy meal. The buttermilk provides a tangy contrast to the sweet, juicy blueberries.

Preparation time **15 minutes + churning**
Total cooking time **5 minutes**
Serves 4

350 g (11¹/4 oz) blueberries
125 g (4 oz) caster sugar
250 ml (8 fl oz) buttermilk
juice of 1 lemon, or to taste
1 egg white

1 Place the blueberries, sugar and 125 ml (4 fl oz) water in a saucepan. Stir over medium heat until the sugar dissolves. Bring to the boil, remove from the heat and allow to cool slightly. Using a metal or wooden spoon, press the mixture through a sieve to make a pulp, discarding the contents of the sieve. Alternatively, purée the mixture in a food processor, then press the pulp through a sieve.

2 Stir the buttermilk into the fruit pulp and add the lemon juice. In a separate bowl, lightly whisk the egg white with a fork until frothy, then stir into the blueberry and buttermilk mixture. Transfer to an ice-cream machine and churn until frozen and smooth. Serve immediately in chilled glasses.

Chef's tips If you do not have an ice-cream machine, pour the mixture into a shallow metal container, freeze until crystals form, then whisk or stir with a fork and return to the freezer. Repeat until frozen evenly and firm.

This sorbet is best enjoyed on the day it is made, but will also freeze for up to 1 week in an airtight container.

Any berries may be substituted for the blueberries, or you could use a combination of berries to make a 'fruits of the forest' buttermilk sorbet. Frozen berries may also be substituted: defrost and drain before use.

For a chunkier sorbet, lightly break up the fruit with a fork in step 1, rather than pressing it through a sieve.

Lemon sabayonette with fresh berries

The name of this superb dessert is derived from the French word for 'zabaglione'. Like a true zabaglione, a sabayonette is best served on the day it is made.

Preparation time **45 minutes + 1 hour refrigeration**
Total cooking time **25 minutes**
Serves **4–6**

SABAYONETTE
3 eggs
120 g (4 oz) caster sugar
100 ml (3 1/4 fl oz) lemon juice
100 g (3 1/4 oz) unsalted butter, softened

200 g (6 1/2 oz) raspberries
100 g (3 1/4 oz) blueberries
100 g (3 1/4 oz) blackberries
40 g (1 1/4 oz) icing sugar
4 sprigs of fresh mint, to decorate

1 To make the sabayonette, half fill a large pan with water and heat until simmering. Have ready a heatproof bowl that will fit over the pan without touching the water. Place the eggs, sugar and lemon juice in the bowl and set it over the simmering water. Whisk until foamy, then constantly whisk for 20–25 minutes, or until the mixture is thick and light yellow and leaves a trail as it falls from the whisk.

2 Remove the bowl from the heat and whisk in the butter, about a teaspoon at a time. Strain into a clean bowl placed over ice, then whisk for 15 minutes, or until very cold. Remove from the ice and chill for at least 1 hour, or until ready to serve.

3 Set aside the four nicest berries of each type of fruit; toss the rest with the icing sugar. Fill the bottom quarter of four large wine glasses or champagne flutes with sabayonette, then spoon some fruit on top. Cover with a second layer of sabayonette and fruit, finishing with a final layer of sabayonette. Arrange the reserved berries on top and garnish with a sprig of mint. Chill until ready to serve.

Fraisier

This is a wonderful gateau for an elegant picnic, or to end a light summer meal. If pink marzipan is not available, knead a few drops of red food colouring through the marzipan until the colour is uniform.

*Preparation time **1 hour 50 minutes + cooling***
*Total cooking time **40 minutes***
Serves 6–8

✿ ✿ ✿

GENOESE SPONGE

3 eggs

I egg yolk

110 g (3³/4 oz) caster sugar

110 g (3³/4 oz) plain flour

10 g (¹/4 oz) unsalted butter, melted and cooled

SYRUP

90 g (3 oz) sugar

25 ml (³/4 fl oz) Kirsch

CREME MOUSSELINE

250 ml (8 fl oz) milk

I vanilla pod

60 g (2 oz) caster sugar

2 egg yolks

20 g (³/4 oz) plain flour

20 g (³/4 oz) cornflour

I tablespoon Kirsch

125 g (4 oz) unsalted butter, softened

500 g (I lb) strawberries, hulled

50 g (1³/4 oz) sieved strawberry jam

100 g (3¹/4 oz) pink marzipan

1 Preheat the oven to moderate 180°C (350°F/Gas 4). To make the Genoese sponge, whisk the eggs, egg yolk and sugar in a bowl over a pan or bowl of hot steaming water until it leaves a trail. Remove from the heat and whisk until cold. Sift the flour, fold it into the mixture, then fold in the melted butter. Pour into a lightly greased 20 x 5 cm (8 x 2 inch) springform ring and bake for 20–25 minutes, or until the sponge shrinks in from the side of the pan. Run a knife inside the ring to release the sponge, then cool on a wire rack. Slice the cold sponge lengthways into two halves and set aside.

2 To make the syrup, dissolve the sugar in 65 ml (2¹/4 fl oz) water in a pan over low heat. Bring to the boil and boil for 1 minute, then stir in the Kirsch and allow to cool.

3 To make the crème mousseline, bring the milk and vanilla pod to the boil. In a bowl, whisk the sugar and egg yolks until pale, then stir in the flours. Strain the milk into the yolk mixture, whisking constantly. Return to the pan and beat rapidly over medium heat until thickened, then boil for 1 minute, stirring constantly. Remove from the heat to cool completely. Add the Kirsch and gradually beat in the butter, whisking well between each addition.

4 Set aside a strawberry for decoration. Halve a third of the strawberries and quarter the rest. To assemble the cake, place a sponge-half in the springform ring (make sure the ring is clean), baked-side-down. Brush with some syrup, spread with a little jam and some of the mousseline. Place the halved strawberries around the outer edge of the cake, the cut sides facing out.

5 Spoon the mousseline into a piping bag fitted with a 1 cm (¹/2 inch) nozzle. Pipe into the gaps between the strawberries. Arrange the remaining strawberries over the sponge, then cover with the remaining mousseline. Smooth the surface and gently press the other sponge on top.

6 Remove the springform ring. Brush on more syrup and thinly spread with jam. Dust a work area with icing sugar, roll out the marzipan to a circle 3 mm (¹/8 inch) thick, and cut a circle with the springform ring. Lift the marzipan onto the cake and smooth the top. Heat the remaining jam, dip in the whole strawberry and place it on top of the cake.

Gratin of summer berries

Beneath a luscious froth of sabayon, quickly grilled until golden brown, lies an assortment of fresh, sweet berries for a delectable summer dessert.

Preparation time **20 minutes**
Total cooking time **20 minutes**
Serves 4

600 g (1 1/4 lb) mixed berries, such as strawberries, blueberries, raspberries and blackberries
2 eggs
2 egg yolks
80 g (2 3/4 oz) caster sugar
1 tablespoon Kirsch

1 Wash the strawberries, dry well, discard the stalks and cut each strawberry in half. Sort the remaining berries to ensure they are all fresh. Arrange the fruit on four ovenproof plates or individual shallow dishes.

2 Half fill a large pan with water and heat until simmering. Have ready a heatproof bowl that will fit over the pan without actually touching the water.

3 To make the sabayon, place the eggs, egg yolks, sugar and Kirsch in the bowl, then place the bowl over the pan of simmering water, ensuring the base of the bowl is not touching the water. Whisk for 10–15 minutes, or until the mixture is thick and creamy and leaves a trail as it falls from the whisk.

4 Preheat the grill to high. Spoon the sabayon over the berries and quickly grill until the sabayon is brown all over. Serve immediately.

Chef's tip The plates of fruit can be arranged in advance. Cover the plates with plastic wrap so the berries do not dry out.

Chef's techniques

◆

Making lamb stock

Ask your butcher to chop the lamb bones so they will fit in your saucepan.

Put 1.5 kg (3 lb) of lamb bones in a large stockpot. Cover with water and bring to the boil. Drain and rinse the bones.

Return the bones to a clean saucepan and add 1 quartered onion, 2 carrots, 1 leek and 1 celery stick, all chopped, as well as 3 litres of water, 1 bouquet garni and 6 peppercorns.

Bring to the boil, reduce the heat and simmer for 2–3 hours, skimming the fat and scum from the surface regularly. A flat strainer is easiest to use for skimming.

Ladle the bones and vegetables into a fine sieve over a bowl. Press the bones and vegetables with the ladle to extract all the liquid. Refrigerate for several hours and remove the solidified fat. Makes about 1.5 litres.

Boning a leg quarter

Tunnel boning, shown here, creates a pocket in one end, which is also ideal for holding a stuffing.

Starting at the thigh end and using a sharp knife, find the thigh bone and run the point of the knife along the top and inside of the bone to release the meat.

Continue down along the bone, scraping down and around to the joint: the meat will gradually turn inside out. Ease the meat off the joint, pulling the boned meat back firmly, being careful not to cut through to the skin.

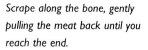

Scrape along the bone, gently pulling the meat back until you reach the end.

Holding the bone and meat firmly, pull hard to remove the bone. You may need the knife to help release any tough tendons. Turn the meat inside out to its original shape.

Removing lobster tail meat

This simple technique makes it easy to present the lobster tail meat in neat, elegant portions.

Turn the lobster on its tail. Using a pair of kitchen scissors, cut lengthways down each side of the belly.

Pull the soft undershell back, exposing the meat of the lobster tail.

Pull the tail meat from the shell, keeping it in a single piece.

Preparing a crab

This method can be used on most crabs. Mud crab, shown here, needs extra care as the shell is very hard.

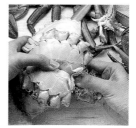

Twist the claws to remove them. Use your thumb as a lever to prise off the hard top shell. Scoop out any creamy brown meat and reserve. Wash and dry the shell well.

Discard the soft stomach sac from the main body of the crab and remove the grey spongy fingers (gills). Scrape out and reserve any more creamy brown meat.

Cut the main body of the crab in half lengthways, then remove the white meat from the body using the end of a teaspoon or fork.

Tying asparagus

Tying a bunch of asparagus makes it easier to handle during cooking.

Grasp the asparagus bunch in the centre. Holding the end of a string with thumb and finger, wrap the string around the upper part three times, cross over and wrap the lower part three times. Secure with a knot.

Bouquet garni

Add the flavour and aroma of herbs to your dish with a freshly made bouquet garni.

Wrap the green part of a leek loosely around a bay leaf, a sprig of thyme, some celery leaves and a few stalks of parsley, then tie with string. Leave a long tail to the string for easy removal.

Published in 1998 by Merehurst Limited, Ferry House, 51–57 Lacy Road, Putney, London SW15 1PR.

Merehurst Limited, Murdoch Books and Le Cordon Bleu thank the 32 masterchefs of all the Le Cordon Bleu Schools, whose knowledge and expertise have made this book possible, especially: Chef Cliche (MOF), Chef Terrien, Chef Boucheret, Chef Duchêne (MOF), Chef Guillut, Chef Steneck, Paris; Chef Males, Chef Walsh, Chef Hardy, London; Chef Chantefort, Chef Bertin, Chef Jambert, Chef Honda, Tokyo; Chef Salembien, Chef Boutin, Chef Harris, Sydney; Chef Lawes, Adelaide; Chef Guiet, Chef Denis, Ottawa. Of the many students who helped the Chefs test each recipe, a special mention to graduates David Welch and Allen Wertheim. A very special acknowledgment to Directors Susan Eckstein, Great Britain, and Kathy Shaw, Paris, who have been responsible for the coordination of the Le Cordon Bleu team throughout this series.

Managing Editor: Kay Halsey
Series Concept, Design and Art Direction: Juliet Cohen
Editor: Katri Hilden
Food Director: Jody Vassallo
Food Editor: Dimitra Stais
Designer: Wing Ping Tong
Photographer: Joe Filshie
Food Stylist: Carolyn Fienberg
Food Preparation: Jo Forrest
Chef's Techniques Photographer: Reg Morrison
Home Economists: Michelle Earl, Michelle Lawton, Kerrie Mullins, Justine Poole, Kerrie Ray, Margot Smithyman

Creative Director: Marylouise Brammer
International Sales Director: Mark Newman
CEO & Publisher: Anne Wilson

ISBN 1 85391 795 8

Printed by Toppan Printing (S) Pte Ltd
First Printed 1998
©Design and photography Murdoch Books® 1998
©Text Le Cordon Bleu 1998
A catalogue record for this book is available from the British Library.

Distributed in the UK by D Services, 6 Euston Street, Freemen's Common, Leicester LE2 7SS Tel 0116-254-7671 Fax 0116-254-4670.
Distributed in Canada by Whitecap (Vancouver) Ltd, 351 Lynn Avenue, North Vancouver, BC V7J 2C4 Tel 604-980-9852 Fax 604-980-8197 or Whitecap (Ontario) Ltd, 47 Coldwater Road, North York, ON M3B 1Y8 Tel 416-444-3442 Fax 416-444-6630
Published and distributed in Australia by Murdoch Books®, 45 Jones Street, Ultimo NSW 2007

The Publisher and Le Cordon Bleu thank Carole Sweetnam for her help with this series and Cydonia the Glass Studio, House, The Glass Artist Gallery, Home & Garden on the Mall, The Pacific East India Company and Villeroy & Boch for assisting photography. Front cover: Asparagus, artichoke and lobster salad.

IMPORTANT INFORMATION

CONVERSION GUIDE

1 cup = 250 ml (8 fl oz)
1 Australian tablespoon = 20 ml (4 teaspoons)
1 UK tablespoon = 15 ml (3 teaspoons)

NOTE: We have used 20 ml tablespoons. If you are using a 15 ml tablespoon, for most recipes the difference will be negligible. For recipes using baking powder, gelatine, bicarbonate of soda and flour, add an extra teaspoon for each tablespoon specified.

CUP CONVERSIONS—DRY INGREDIENTS

1 cup flour, plain or self-raising = 125 g (4 oz)
1 cup sugar, caster = 250 g (8 oz)
1 cup breadcrumbs, dry = 125 g (4 oz)

IMPORTANT: Those who might be at risk from the effects of salmonella food poisoning (the elderly, pregnant women, young children and those suffering from immune deficiency diseases) should consult their GP with any concerns about eating raw eggs.